"Time travel, ancient legends, and
seductive romance are seamlessly
interwoven into one captivating package."
—*Publishers Weekly* on Midnight's Master

"Dark, sexy, magical. When I want
to indulge in a sizzling fantasy adventure,
I read Donna Grant."
—Allison Brennan, *New York Times* bestseller

5 Stars! Top Pick! "An absolute must read!
From beginning to end,
it's an incredible ride."
—*Night Owl Reviews*

"It's good vs. evil Druid in the next
installment of Grant's Dark Warrior series.
The stakes get higher as discerning one's
true loyalties become harder. Grant's
compelling characters and continued
presence of previous protagonists are key
reasons why these books are so gripping.
Another exciting and thrilling chapter!"
—*RT Book Reviews* on Midnight's Lover

"Donna Grant has given the paranormal
genre a burst of fresh air..."
—*San Francisco Book Review*

Don't miss these other
spellbinding novels by
DONNA GRANT

CONSTANTINE
A HISTORY

THE DARK KINGS

DONNA GRANT

This is a work of fiction. All of the characters,
organizations, and events portrayed in this novel
are either products of the author's imagination or
are used fictitiously.

Constantine: A History
© **2017 by DL Grant, LLC**
Excerpt from Dark Alpha's Embrace copyright ©
2015 by Donna Grant

Cover design © 2017 by
Charity Hendry

ISBN 13: 978-1942017431

www.DonnaGrant.com
www.MotherofDragonsBooks.com

Available in ebook and print editions

For Liz-

For your friendship, shopping trips, food, and hours of talk about the Dragon Kings.

DARK KINGS

Dear Reader,

Sometimes, it's hard for me, even as a writer, to find words to express how much I love and appreciate all of you taking this journey with me through 41+ books (with more to come) in the Dark World.

Some of you began with the Warriors and Druids in the Dark Sword series. Some came on board with the Dark Warriors series. And still more with the Dark Kings.

But then again, who can resist Dragon Kings, right?

Having recently returned from RT (Romantic Times Convention), one of the questions that kept coming up (besides who is Rhi's DK?) was: Do I really need to read the Reaper series?

My response to that is that, no, you

don't have to. But I highly recommend it. Why? Because the Dragon Kings – and Rhi – show up in these books more and more. There are going to be big tie-ins coming, just as there were with the Warriors/Druids and the Dragon Kings. There are reasons why Death wants Rhi followed by one of the Reapers, and why Death takes such an interest in the Dragon Kings – massive, whopping reasons.

Now, I think everyone knows my love of my Dragon Kings. I'd wanted to write dragons for years and kept being told no. Then, when I was asked to spin off the DS/DW world, I immediately said dragons. And my editor agreed.

I can't tell you how much – and loudly – I celebrated that day. I was finally going to be able to write about my Dragon Kings that I had been dreaming of for years! (There might have been some champagne drunk and perhaps even some dancing around the house.)

While I refuse to give away spoilers, I've always said that Con would get his own book, and that it would be the last book in the series. So, before his book releases, I thought this would be a good time for you to get a behind-the-scenes look at the King of Dragon Kings. I want you, my dedicated dragon lovers, to see another side of Con, a private side he doesn't share.

With anyone.

Because...well, you'll see when you read the story.

I also wanted to go more in-depth into the history of the Dragon Kings. There is so much to tell, and a lot of it is backstory that would weigh a book down. Hence, Constantine: A History.

It wasn't my plan to do the Reaper series. I was asked by my publisher to do another spin-off, and for a bit, I wondered what I could ever come up with that could compare with dragons? Then it hit me. What other beings play such an integral part of the Dark World?

Why Fae, of course.

The Dark portray the villains to utter perfection, but what if they weren't all bad guys? That question led me down a slew of others. I wanted to know more about the Fae culture and how they lived. I wanted to know their hurts, their pain, their desires, their grievances, their hopes, and their love.

Once I thought about the Fae being Reapers and bringing in both Light and Dark, as well as getting to see the Fae in a different sense than we do with the DKs, I dove into the series with so much anticipation that the first story came faster than I could write it.

With each Reaper story I write, I come to love them more and more. (Yes, I do have a favorite. I might tell you if you ply me with wine.) If you've not delved into the Reaper world, I hope by the time you finish reading this story of Con's past that you'll give the Reapers a go.

Through the Dragon King books,

we've seen Con in many different lights, and, for me, that's what makes him so damn amazing. And human – in many instances. I'm hoping with this story that you'll learn a little more about the King of Kings, and, with any luck, start to fall in love with him as I have.

With much love,
DG

*The 12th of August,
human year 1601
Dreagan*

    *As I write this, I cannot help but look
back over the years. The date the mortals
use means nothing to me, or any of the
other Dragon Kings. Yet, we are bound by
it, if we are to live in their world.*

    A world I helped to create.

    A world my kind must now hide in.

    *I finished visiting those Dragon Kings
who have chosen to sleep. It is a burden I
gladly take on to give my brethren a
chance to escape the hellish lives we have
chosen to live. After all these untold
thousands of years that rain around me
like the stars above, it doesn't get any*

easier.

I soldier on, as do the other Kings. Because we hold out hope that one day we'll be able to bring our dragons home again.

Even as I impart the past decade of information to the sleeping Kings, I know there is one thought that never leaves them. When can they see their dragons again? I wish I had an answer.

But even as all of the magic on this realm flows through me, I have no solution.

V was the last Dragon King I saw. I sat beside him as he slept, but I could still feel his rage for what the humans had done to him. For V – and aye, even for Ulrik – the answer is simple. Show the mortals who we really are. Resume our rightful place as rulers of the realm with magic and might.

But how can I? After every King swore to protect the defenseless, magic-less mortals?

There is no remedy. Just as I feel the magic draining from this world, I wonder how long before we can remain hidden. Before we have no choice but to show the humans that dragons are a part of their world.

Before we're once more at war.

Though I will try and tell the mortals there is no weapon they have that can destroy us, I know they will not listen. Still, I will attempt to save them – even though I know the end result will be their demise.

There is no winning for either side, but especially not for us Dragon Kings. Not now, and I fear not ever.

Constantine, the King of Golds
King of Dragon Kings

Con set aside his quill and let the ink dry. He blew out a breath and raked a hand through his hair, shoving it from his face and gathering it at the base of his neck before wrapping a strip of leather around the thick length.

Dawn was fast approaching. He softly closed the journal and tucked it away in a drawer of his desk before rising. As he walked from his office, he proudly looked around at what the Kings had accomplished living in secret. Their whisky had become so well known that even Queen Elizabeth requested it. Con had plans for their company's future, and everything was already falling into place.

The whisky, as well as the sheep and cattle, were a viable cover for the Kings that could be used for hundreds of years to come. And Con planned to work it until it was no longer needed.

He reached the bottom floor and found Nikolai surrounded by candles as he painted another dragon scene. This one was from the Fae Wars. It was a reminder that even though the Kings hid from the humans, they still fought to protect them. But how much longer would Con be able to convince his brethren to do that? Already he'd lost Ulrik....

"We know where he resides," Nikolai said.

Con swung his gaze away from the canvas to look into Nikolai's light blue eyes. He didn't pretend not to know that Nikolai spoke about Ulrik. "Nay."

"I think you should talk to him."

Talk. Ulrik would most likely try to take his head. No, it was better that Con keep his distance. He'd reframed from killing Ulrik once, and he didn't want to be put in the position where he had no choice in the matter.

Nikolai let out a loud sigh and nodded his head of auburn hair. "I understand."

Con clapped his friend on the shoulder before walking past him and out the door. As soon as he was outside, he drew in a deep breath. There would never come a day where he ever went far from Dreagan. It wasn't just the seat of power for the King of Dragon Kings, it was his home.

He spent the next few hours leisurely walking the grounds watching the sun slowly rise in the sky. More time was devoted to helping Cain with a herd of cattle. Con then filled a few hours watching the dogs work the sheep from one pasture to another. After that, he checked on each process of the making of whisky.

The next time he glanced at the sun, it was noon. Something made

Con turn toward the village instead of the manor, where he always took his meals. While he might visit The Fox and The Hound pub that Laith ran for a pint or two, it was a rare occasion. He liked that the other Kings took it upon themselves to keep close to the humans, because it saved him from having to do it.

Yet, Con's feet took him toward the village and Laith's pub. Because he kept out of the public eye, Con didn't have to worry about a new identity for fear of being recognized. He walked into the establishment and let his gaze roam over the occupants.

No one looked his way. Pleased, Con strolled to the bar where he spotted Laith. The King of Blacks raised a brow in question. Con merely shrugged as he took a seat.

"Everything all right?" Laith asked, his forehead creased in concern. "No' that I'm no' pleased to see you here."

Con rested his arms on the bar. "Something drew me."

Laith straightened, instantly on alert as his head swiveled to look around the pub. "I doona feel any magic except for ours."

"I doona believe it's magic. Just a feeling. So, be at ease."

Laith snorted. "That isna possible, Con, and hasna been since we sent our dragons away."

"Doona give up hope that they will return one day."

"Have you?"

Con held his gaze before Laith gave a shake of his blond head, his long hair reaching past his shoulders. Without another word, Laith put a dram of whisky before him and walked away to tend to another customer.

Con wrapped his fingers around the glass and swirled the liquid to let the oxygen reach the whisky to bring out all the aromas. He took in the deep amber color. Then he brought it to his lips. He inhaled the spicy, rich scent, feeling it deep within him. Only after did he allow a little to fill his mouth. He closed his eyes and let the delicious, smooth taste slide down his throat.

Damn, but Dreagan whisky was amazing.

He finished the Scotch and motioned for another before ordering a Sheppard's pie to eat. Con remained on the stool, and was surprised to find that he enjoyed himself. The conversations of the humans barely registered. He gazed around at a community that he protected, a village that thrived next to Dreagan.

Everyone from Dreagan was always welcome in the village, and Con didn't want to think about what might happen if those same mortals learned that the occupants of the estate were really dragons. For now, humans believed dragons were nothing more than myths – and Con intended for that to remain.

"You enjoy this," Con said to Laith when he approached.

Laith grinned as his gaze moved from one side of the tavern to the other and lowered his voice. "I've had this pub for two hundred years, and you want to ask me this now?"

"I asked when you first built it. I'm asking again."

"It gives us a presence here, which we need."

Con nodded slowly. "And how do the villagers see us?"

Laith leaned on the bar. "They like us, if that's what you want to know."

"It's helpful, aye, but I want to know if they suspect?"

"No' at all," Laith replied. "We've done too good of a job for them ever to discover the truth."

At least there was that. Con paid for his drinks and food and gave a wave to Laith before setting off to return to Dreagan.

He only got a short distance before he spotted a woman in all black standing next to a horse pulling a cart that had a few meager belongings inside. The woman lifted one of the animal's back legs and was looking at its hoof.

Unsure why, Con found himself drawn to her. He walked closer, moving slowly until she lifted her head. He held up his hands to show her he meant no harm and halted.

"Can I help you with anything?"

She gently lowered the horse's leg and straightened. He got a good look at her. While on the petite side, her glossy black locks gathered into a long plait that hung over her shoulder. Unusual lavender eyes captured him instantly. Only then did he see the unmistakable beauty of her face.

He made himself take in the poor material of her garments, but he had the suspicion that the woman was anything but common. With a narrowed gaze, he tried to sense any magic around her and found none.

For a moment, he thought she might be a Fae using glamour to hide her silver eyes. Or red eyes if she were a Dark Fae.

"My mare threw a shoe," the woman said as she dusted off her hands.

Con heard the faint dialect in her speech that couldn't be covered by the Scots accent, but he couldn't quite place it. He parted his lips, intending to tell her where to find the local blacksmith. Except that wasn't what came out of his mouth. Instead, he said, "I can get that fixed for you."

"And you are?" she asked, raising a slim, black brow.

If he had any doubt as to her nobility, the fact she would talk to him in such a way all but proclaimed it. "Constantine," he replied with a bow of his head.

"I'm Heather," she said with a smile. "Are you a blacksmith?"

"Nay, however, my estate has one."

Both brows rose as she looked at him. "Are you a lord then?"

He hid his smile as she took in the fine breeches, shirt, and vest that he wore. "Nothing of the sort. I merely inherited land from family."

"That usually goes hand in hand with a title."

"I've no need for titles."

She regarded him silently for a moment. "Nay, I don't believe you do. You're one of those rare men who doesn't care about such trivial things."

He didn't bother to correct her. How could he begin to explain that he had wanted to be King of Dragon Kings for as long as he could remember? And he had done whatever was needed to ensure the position was his.

But he didn't care for was mortal designation they seemed obsessed with. The humans could buy, bribe, or blackmail their way into a title. The magic within the realm chose who would be a Dragon King. And only the strongest of each clan, the dragon with the most magic, could challenge the present King for the spot.

"Where is this estate?" she asked softly.

Con nodded to the left. "It's a wee bit of a walk."

"You say that as if I look to be fearful of such exercise."

He smiled despite himself. "I'd never suggest such a thing."

"That's wise," she replied with a grin.

"Shall we?" he asked as he held out an arm.

Heather took the mare's bridle and softly called, giving a little pull to get the horse walking. Except the mare would not stop looking at Con. He walked to the animal, talking softly to it all the while. When he reached her, he stroked down her velvety nose before allowing the horse to sniff him.

Despite being a dragon in disguise, animals always instinctively knew he and his kind were masters over the land. While in human form, creatures of all kinds were drawn to the Kings.

Finally satisfied, the mare blew out a breath. Con took a step back and nodded to Heather who got the horse walking. They moved slowly, Con's mind sorting through everything. There was something about her that left him off-balance. While she was one of the most beautiful women he ever laid eyes on, that wasn't it.

Although he couldn't detect any magic, he suspected she was something more than a mere mortal. He'd been around enough humans to know. Nor was she a Druid, because even the most skilled Druid couldn't hide her magic – nor did they try.

If Heather wasn't a mortal, Druid, or Fae, then what was she?

"You look perplexed."

He glanced at over to find her staring at him. Con clasped his hands behind him and shrugged. "Women doona often travel alone."

"You're concern for my welfare is appreciated, but you needn't worry."

Con was almost tempted to shift and see if that could frighten her, because it appeared nothing could break the steely spine of the comely Heather.

"So you know how to defend yourself?" he asked.

With her gaze straight ahead, she replied in a cool voice, "I do."

For a reason he couldn't fathom, she fascinated him. Con tried to pinpoint the cause, but he kept coming up empty handed. It was a rare event to find a mortal with a lethal combination of beauty, wit, and brains. If she really could fight, that added another element that just wasn't found.

In a Fae, definitely.

There might even be a Druid or two who came close to this mortal, but Con couldn't be sure.

"You don't know what to make of me, do you?" Heather said as she shot him a smile.

"I doona," he replied, not bothering to lie.

She laughed, the sound soft and musical. To his surprise, Con found his lips curling into a smile. Since it was something he didn't do often, he was shocked this woman could manage what none of his brethren had in...well, in thousands of years.

Heather licked her lips as her smile faded. "Who are you, Constantine?"

"Why do you ask that?" he queried, instantly on guard.

"Because you appear to have the weight of the world on your shoulders."

He turned his head to her. "If we're going to ask such personal questions, I pose the same to you. Because, dear Heather, you are no' all that you seem."

Instead of becoming angry, she grinned at him, her lavender eyes flashing with mirth. "Oh, I'm simply a woman trying to make her way in the world."

"Ah, but you're no' simply anything."

"The same could be said of you,"

she replied succinctly.

Con tipped his head at her. Conversations such as these never occurred with mortals, and while he knew he would be better cutting such words off, he found he wanted to continue the banter.

And there was even a small part of him – a very tiny drop – that thought about showing her exactly who he was. That was foolishness, however, and he halted such thoughts immediately.

"Why do you think that? I'm no different than other men."

Heather smiled and shook her head. "Those are words meant for a fool, and I am no fool."

"Meaning?" he pressed.

She halted and turned to him. The jingling of the bridle filled the air as the horse and cart stopped with her. "On my journey, I've encountered a fair number of individuals from the most lowly slave, to beggars, regular folk, nobility, and even royalty. I've looked into each of their eyes. Not once did I find what I see in your black eyes."

"What is that?" he asked before he could stop himself.

He imagined she might say hopelessness, despair, or even despondency.

"Vitality."

Con frowned, completely taken aback.

She took a step closer. "I also see strength. You have that in abundance."

"Who are you?" he demanded.

"A woman who has an injured horse."

He shook his head and let his arms drop to his sides. Just before he pressed her for more, he hesitated. Whoever this woman was, she didn't seem to know he was a Dragon King, but she sensed he was something more. If he pressured her for more information, she would do the same for him.

Perhaps it was better if he left well enough alone.

They resumed their walk, this time in silence. All the while, he discreetly studied her. Heather carried herself like a woman used to doing things her own way. While he saw no weapons on her person, that didn't mean there weren't some hidden or nearby.

Hell, for all he knew, *she* was a weapon.

Con replayed her words in his head. She teased and cajoled easily, but when he glanced at her now staring ahead, her face devoid of mirth, he caught a glimpse of apprehension about her.

It was fleeting. Most likely something she hid even from herself, but it had him wondering what could bother her so. It angered him that he really wanted to know. He wanted to help her, but for the life of him, he couldn't figure out why.

He didn't trust her, which meant he should keep her at arm's length. Why then, did he have a sense that he should offer his aid in more than shoeing her horse?

Ahead were the gates of Dreagan. She perked up and spoke to the horse when she spotted them. No longer did she try to engage him in conversation. It was obvious she was used to being alone, because she was quite content with her own company. He understood that. While there was always Dragon Kings awake, Con mostly kept to himself.

Not because he didn't love his brethren. It was because there were many secrets he had to keep – and wounds deep upon his soul he was trying to live with. It was better done in solitude. Besides, the Kings looked to him for answers. He couldn't bring doubt into their minds by sharing his worries and fears. Of all of them, he was the one who needed to stand strong and unwavering.

Once they reached the barn, Con tried to help her unhitch the horse, but Heather waved him off. He watched her for a moment before he turned on his heel and went to find Roman.

The King of Pale Blue dragons was sorting through various metals before him. He looked up as Con approached and gave a nod of his sandy blond head and faced him. "Kellan found some new metals I'm about to test out."

Con eyed the stack. While Kellan's power was finding metals, it was Roman who had the ability to control any metal to form whatever shape he wanted. "I'm curious to see what you create."

"Aye. But that's not what brought you to me." Roman's green eyes held his. "What is it?"

"I encountered a woman on the road."

A blond brow shot up. "You left Dreagan?"

"Aye. I visited the pub."

At that, both brows rose. Roman crossed his arms over his chest and widened his feet. "No' only did you leave Dreagan, but you went to Laith's pub? *And* you spoke to a female?"

"Bloody hell," Con ground out as he glanced toward the ceiling of the barn. "You make it sound as if such occurrences are cause for concern."

"With you they are."

Con drew in a deep breath. "I like to keep all of you on your toes."

"You do that verra well," Roman said with a grin. "Now, I gather you didna come here to tell me of your exploits today."

Con prayed for patience. Of course, Roman would think he'd had a dalliance with the woman, because why else would Con talk to her? He squeezed the bridge of his nose with his thumb and forefinger before dropping his arm.

"You didna bed her?" Roman asked, surprised.

"Nay, I didna."

"Was she pretty?"

"Beautiful." Con had no idea why he said that.

Roman smiled. "If you doona want her, then I might have a go."

Con stepped to the side and held out his arm. "Be my guest."

"She's here?" Roman replied in a shocked whisper.

Con nodded slowly. "Her horse threw a shoe."

Roman's smile was gone as he looked from Con to the doorway. After a hesitation, he strode from the barn. Con followed, hiding his grin when Roman drew up short.

"Hello," Heather said as she patted the mare.

Roman stood staring at her as if he'd never encountered such beauty before, and to be honest, they hadn't – unless you counted the Fae.

Con came to stand beside him. "Heather, this is Roman. He'll be happy to shoe the mare."

"Thank you," Heather replied, flashing a bright smile to Roman.

Roman bowed his head. "It'll be my pleasure."

When Roman had taken the bridle from Heather's hand, Con turned his attention to her. "Are you hungry?"

"I could eat," she said.

He walked her to the manor, watching as her gaze darted about taking it all in. Dreagan was his pride and joy – as it was to all Dragon Kings. Every one of them had a hand in creating and building everything on the land.

"I have no words to describe the beauty of this place."

Con's chest puffed out. Once inside the manor, he observed her as she moved from one painting to another, scrutinizing each. He wondered if she would notice all the dragons around the manor, but if she did, she didn't say anything. And perhaps that was for the best. It would mean he would need to come up with some excuse, and he didn't want to lie to her.

On the way to the library, Con motioned to one of the servants to bring food. Within the walls of the massive room, he sank into a chair before the cold fireplace and found his gaze on Heather once again.

She moved around the room, her fingers trailing along the spines of the books with her head tilted to read the titles. The longer he was with her, the more he really wanted to know who she was. Or maybe he only yearned for her to be more than a mortal. Maybe he was searching for something that wasn't there.

That was most likely due to his loneliness. Not that he would admit that to anyone. The spell the Kings put upon themselves never to feel anything for humans was still in place after their betrayal to Ulrik. The treachery also made him extra guarded around women.

Or it usually did. It wasn't so with Heather.

Con turned his head to the window. Would a day go by where he didn't think about what happened to his closest friend? Of how it had turned Ulrik so dark that he began a war with the humans? Con was well aware that his actions of binding Ulrik's magic and banishing him from Dreagan would be one of his greatest regrets.

But Ulrik left him no choice. As King of Dragon Kings, Con had to think about everyone, not just one King or dragon. He had to set aside his personal feelings, and even then, he almost hadn't been able to do it.

"What has you so sad?"

Con drew in a breath when he realized Heather now stood at the chair opposite him. "The past."

"Ah," she replied softly. "The past can have the power to destroy if you allow it."

"Yet, it is the past that defines us."

"A past is just that, a past. It may shape who you are now, but that doesn't mean you should allow it to hold you as it does."

He slid his gaze to her. "You speak as if from knowledge."

"Yes."

The word was said like a whisper. Heather then looked out the window, staring at the sun-soaked glen as sheep lazily munched on the grass. After a moment, she lowered herself into the chair.

"Did you let go of the past?" Con asked.

When she looked at him, a smile in place, he noticed that it was forced. But it was the regret and pain in her gaze that struck him like a punch to the chest.

"I'm working on it," she admitted.

Con turned his hands over, spreading his fingers and gazed down at his palms. "I'm no' sure I can."

"If you don't, it'll obliterate you. And everything you've built here."

His gaze snapped up to her. "Meaning?"

Her wide-eyed innocent look was believable as she said. "Look around at this beautiful home. You may have inherited it, but you're maintaining it. Dreagan is an amazing place. I would hate for you to lose it because of something in the past."

Con studied her a long, silent moment. He couldn't tell if she was being coy and choosing her words carefully or if she really didn't know anything. It was a big chance he was taking in not making a decision, but he knew he couldn't live with the weight of her death if he killed her and she was an innocent.

But if she knew something...he could be putting Dreagan and every Dragon King in jeopardy.

Not that they couldn't take care of themselves, but Con didn't want another war – not with the Fae, humans, or anyone else. He was tired of fighting. But he was also tired of hiding.

Still, if a war with the mortals started up again, he knew the Dark Fae would see an opportunity to attack either the Kings or the mortals. That would mean an attack on two sides.

Then there was Ulrik. He may no longer have his magic, but he was still immortal and carrying a deep hatred for Con. There was little doubt in his mind that Ulrik would also take the chance and attack.

Con wasn't sure if he could count on the Light Fae for support. Usaeil, the Queen of the Fae, joined him in the past, but that meant nothing now.

"I've said something to upset you," Heather said. She lowered her head. "My apologies. I meant no offence."

"I'm verra careful of the people I allow on Dreagan, and even more cautious of having strangers know my business."

She met his gaze and put her hand over her heart. "I'm honored you allowed me to see the splendor of your home. Let me put your mind at ease. I've no interest in knowing whatever business you conduct here."

He raised a brow, listening to each word carefully.

"I spend most of my time in solitude with only my horse for company, and while that doesn't bother me, when I find someone with your intellect who I find interesting, I like the company."

It was a plausible explanation. And he really wanted to believe her.

She gathered her hands in her lap and stood. "If you prefer, I can wait in the barn while Roman is working."

"Nay," Con said and sat up straight, ready to stop her. He was confused by his actions since he had yet to make up his mind about her, but he knew he liked Heather. "Please, stay."

With a soft smile, she sank back

onto the chair.

For better or worse, Con sealed the fate of everyone on Dreagan by asking Heather to remain. He was taking a chance that she didn't have a nefarious purpose. It wasn't normal for him to make such rash decisions. He always looked at each problem or situation at every angle to figure out which was the best course of action.

And yet, he couldn't seem to follow his own patterns when it came to Heather.

"Where are you traveling to?" he asked after the servant had brought in a tray of food.

Heather was quick to take a bite. She chewed and swallowed before she said, "I've no destination in mind. I go where the road takes me."

"Is that no' dangerous?"

"You mean because I'm a woman?" she asked with a grin.

He smiled and nodded in agreement. "Aye. It's something a man would do, and no one would question him."

"So why cannot a woman do the same?"

"I doona have a problem with that, but others doona feel the same."

"I don't understand narrow-mindedness."

Con leaned his head against the high-backed chair. "Neither do I."

"It's silly that a woman shouldn't be able to travel on her own without others looking down on her. I've as much right to the road and the sky above me as any man."

He stretched his legs out, crossing his ankles. "Aye."

"You say that, but you also questioned me."

"I questioned your safety. That isna the same. Bandits are everywhere. They would see you as a prize."

She set down her goblet after taking a drink. "I'd like them to try and attack me."

"Could you defend yourself against three men? Six? More?" When she didn't reply, he continued. "That is why I question you traveling alone."

Licking her lips, Heather leaned back in the chair. "Tell me, would it do me any good if I had another woman with me? What about an elderly man? I would be more concerned about protecting them against such rabble than I would about myself."

"I was thinking more along the lines of a man capable of fighting alongside you."

Her gaze went out the window, but it was the deep longing he saw that made him frown.

She took a breath. "And how would this capable man and I stand against six or more attackers?"

Con linked his fingers together. He couldn't exactly tell her that if she had a

Dragon King with her, no one would even look sideways at her. Because they weren't talking about Dragon Kings. They were discussing mortals. And that was something all together different.

Her head swung to him, tilting a little. "We would fare no better than if I was alone."

"Point taken. However, individuals might think twice about bothering you if you had someone with you."

"It's a chance I take."

"Why?" he pressed, suddenly curious.

She put a piece of meat in her mouth and chewed. "That past I spoke of, my journey is helping me control it instead of it controlling me."

"I take that to mean things are going well?"

"They did for a while. Then there was an...issue that arose. I failed to handle it quickly enough."

Con fisted his hands before laying them on the arms of the chair. "But you did take care of it?"

"If I said no, would you offer to help?" she asked with a small smile.

"I might."

"That is very kind of you, but there is no need. Everything is once more in order."

One of the strings tying his cuffs together came undone. Con sighed in frustration, but did nothing to fix it. Heather moved the tray from her lap and rose. She then dropped down on her knees next to his chair. On instinct, Con pulled his arm away.

"I don't bite," she said with a gleam in her eye and held out her hand.

He wasn't entirely sure she didn't bite, but he was unable to refuse her anything. Con gave her his arm. Her fingers never touched his skin as she quickly tied the ribbon into a bow. In the next moment, she was back in her chair.

"Thank you," he said.

"I imagine those come loose often."

He flattened his lips, hating the ribbon. "Aye."

"You should really think about using something else."

"Fashion isna something I care about."

"Why not?"

He frowned at her. "Why should it be?"

"You say you don't have a title, and yet you run Dreagan. Do you think people would listen to you if you walked about in peasant clothing? They want to know your estate is doing well, which means you need to dress the part." She held out her hand, indicating his current attire. "You say you don't care about fashion, but you're wearing the latest clothing. Not to mention the material is of the highest quality."

Unable to help himself, he chuckled. "You're calling me a liar."

"Well," she said and shrugged. "I think I'd rather say I'm pointing out a fact."

"To be fair, I do wear the clothes of my station."

"But they're not really you."

His emotions were on a pendulum with her. Each time he thought he knew what she might say or do, she surprised him. "And what do you think I should be wearing?"

"I don't know," she said while looking him over with a critical eye. "I don't think you'll know for a long time, but once you figure it out, it'll be yours. You won't care what anyone else is wearing, nor will you listen when someone else tries to tell you to change it."

He cocked his head to the side. "Can you see into the future?"

"I can read people," she replied with a curve of her lips.

"That's a bit more than reading me."

"I like you."

He found himself beginning to smile. "The feeling is mutual."

It was an odd moment, to be sure,

because neither of them meant it in a romantic fashion. The affection between them went beyond to something he couldn't quite name.

Her gaze moved to the books. "Have you read all of these?"

"Aye."

"Somehow that doesn't surprise me," she replied. "There are empty shelves.

He looked to the highest bookshelves. "They will be filled."

"I've no doubt. Are you married?"

He liked her directness. It was refreshing. "Nay."

"Neither am I, nor will I ever be."

"Why is that?"

She flashed him a smile as she stood and walked around the library. "I'm too independent for men."

"No' all men."

"The majority." She shrugged and glanced at him over her shoulder. "I've always been on my own, so it's nothing new."

He sat up and braced his forearms

on his thighs. "I, too, have been alone, but in a different way. I'm surrounded by my brothers, but -"

"You're set apart from them," she said over him.

He looked at her, meeting her lavender gaze. "Aye."

"You don't have to be alone."

"I do," he said and looked to the floor.

Soft footsteps came toward him only to stop before one of the windows. "I've enjoyed my time at Dreagan more than you'll ever know."

With a frown, Con lifted his head. "You speak as if you're leaving."

"No doubt Roman is nearly finished, and I've taken up too much of your time already."

He pushed to his feet and went to stand beside her. "This has been pleasant interlude."

"Immensely so."

They shared a smile before turning to look out the window again. Con couldn't shake off the feeling that he should get to know Heather more. She seemed to discern things about him. Though she never let any hint drop that she knew his secret, there was something about her words and the way she spoke that said she might know more.

Any misgivings he'd had about her dissipated while he had been with her. There had been plenty of opportunities for her to demand something or even threaten him, but she hadn't. The entire time, he felt as if she were his friend, as if they were comrades.

That couldn't possibly be true since he was immortal and had been alive for millions of years. And yet he couldn't dispel the notion.

"I bet this place looks gorgeous in every season," she said.

He clasped his hands behind his back. "It does. Each time I think I've finally found my favorite season, the next one rolls in. I know every inch of this land. I've walked it numerous time."

"It's in your soul."

"Aye."

She looked over to him. "And you are in the land."

The door to the library opened and Roman entered. "All finished."

"I'm most grateful," Heather said as she pivoted and walked to Roman. "How much do I owe you?"

"Nothing." Con moved to join her, not yet ready for her to leave.

She turned her large lavender eyes to him. "Thank you, but I must give you something in return for your hospitality."

"We're glad to help," Roman answered.

With no other choice, Con followed Roman and Heather from the house to the barn. He walked behind them, observing how Heather seemed to put everyone at ease. She had Roman talking within seconds. Con had the insane theory to introduce her to all the Dragon Kings – even V – and see what happened.

When they reached the barn, the mare whinnied as soon as she saw them. Heather rushed to the horse and greeted her with soft words as she stroked the animal's neck.

"Stay for dinner," Con said.

Heather turned her large eyes to him. "An intriguing offer."

"We've excellent food, if I do say so myself," Roman added.

She turned back to the horse. Several moments went by before Heather faced them. "I'm sorry, but I must decline."

"It'll be dusk soon," Roman argued.

"I need to make up the time I've lost."

Con took the mare and led her to the cart where he fastened it to the horse. All the while, Roman was talking to Heather. Con waited for them to finish, and then finally Heather made her way to him.

"You doona have to leave," he told her.

She looked back at Dreagan briefly. "I do, but it won't be forever."

"Will you return this way then?"

"One day."

"Then, I'll look forward to it. Doona let it be too long, lass."

She smiled, chuckling. "Is that a command?"

"Would you listen to it if it was?"

"I'm afraid not."

His lips curved into a smile for the third time that day. "It was worth a try."

He offered his hand to her. When she hesitated to take it, he frowned, wondering why she didn't want to touch him. Then, her small hand slid inside his. He helped her up and handed her the reins.

"Safe journeys, Heather."

"Remember, don't let the past control you. Acknowledge it, but accept what was done and move on. For yourself and your brothers. Farwell,

Constantine. Until we meet again."

She clicked to the horse. Con stepped back as the cart lurched forward. He stared after Heather until she was out of sight. Then he pivoted and returned to the house, making his way back up to his office.

He lowered himself into his chair and leaned back, folding his hands over his stomach. There were a fair number of things he should attend to, but instead, he watched the light coming through the windows move across the floor as the sun sank toward the horizon.

When darkness claimed the land, Con remained in his chair not bothering to light candles. Not that he needed them. Being a Dragon King meant that he could see in darkness and light.

But being a Dragon King also meant that he had to keep himself apart from everyone – no matter if they were human or Fae. He'd accepted his role. Hell, he'd actually embraced it. Or had until today. Spending time, however brief, with Heather had been refreshing.

She intrigued him with her words. She also maddened him with her remarks. Even now he didn't know what she was. Everything pointed to her being mortal, but he wasn't completely convinced.

If she was mortal – or even a Druid – then she couldn't know he was a Dragon King. After hiding and wiping away all evidence of the existence of dragons, Con and the other Kings had worked tirelessly to make sure the humans believed dragons were nothing more than myth.

Now, a Fae would know who he was. That made more sense. Except for the fact that he could detect no magic within her. No matter how skillful the Fae were at using glamour to disguise themselves, nothing masked their magic.

Which brought Con right back to where he began.

He'd gone round and round with his thoughts, trying to determine if he missed something in Heather's words or appearance.

Con had no idea how long he sat there without noticing that someone was at the door. He looked up to find a form leaning against the entrance with his arms crossed. He met Banan's gray eyes.

"I gather you're thinking about our visitor, Heather," Banan said as he dropped his arms and pushed away from the doorway. "She's all Roman can talk about. I'm sorry I missed meeting her."

Con kept his gaze on the King of Dark Blues as Banan walked into the office and took one of the chairs set in front of the desk.

"Roman believes she's mortal."

It wasn't so much Banan's words, but his tone that got Con's attention. "You doona? Despite no' meeting or seeing her?"

Banan blew out a breath. "It's been a verra long time since Ulrik left Dreagan. That day is stamped in every King's memory whether we want it there or no'. Something else none of us can forget is that we swore never to be betrayed by a human again. Enough damage had been done to Ulrik. You came up with the idea to use magic to ensure a mortal would never have such a hold over us again."

"You're point?"

"Roman liked Heather. The spell on us doesna prevent us from recognizing beauty, but it does stop us from such fondness as Roman seems to have for the lass."

Con considered Banan's words for a moment. "There was something about her that I couldna quite make sense of. I felt no magic, and yet I'd swear she wasna human."

"Which would make sense about how Roman – and you – feel about her."

"I've no' encountered a being on this

realm who doesna have magic, but also isna mortal."

Banan shrugged, his lips flattening. "Maybe she's a new being."

"Or one strong enough to mask her magic."

"I'm no' sure how I feel about that," Banan stated, worry lacing his words.

Con opened the mental link that linked all Dragon Kings. *"Everyone on patrol tonight, strengthen the wards around Dreagan. Also, make sure you remain high enough in the sky that no one will be able to spot you."*

Con then rose from his chair and stalked from the office with Banan on his heels. He made his way to the conservatory and the secret door that led into the mountain behind the manor.

The Kings who were awake rotated nightly patrolling the skies around Dreagan. It allowed them to shift into their true forms and fly while also ensuring that Dreagan remain safe.

Con knew the tunnels within the mountain by heart. He knew which Kings favored which caverns when they weren't in their own mountains. He also knew every carving of dragons throughout the mountain since he and Ulrik had started the first one.

But he wasn't thinking about Ulrik this night. The past had no business in this moment. So he took Heather's advice and set it aside. By the time he reached the back of the mountain where there was a massive opening large enough to fit a dragon, he'd made his decision.

"You're going after her," Banan said from behind him.

Con turned his head to the side and yanked on the ribbons clasping the wrists of his shirt. Then he quickly disrobed. With merely a thought, he shifted.

It was glorious to be in his true form. To stretch his wings and feel the fire deep within. His talons scraped along the rock floor. He yearned to feel the wind slip over his gold scales as he glided through the moonlit sky. To twist and turn through the clouds while maneuvering through the currents.

He walked to the opening and looked up at the inky sky. Then he leapt into the air, flapping his wings to catch the air and take him upward. Con made a pass over Dreagan before briefly flying with a few of the patrols.

Then he dipped a wing and swung back around in the direction Heather had been going. She should be easy to find, especially with the fact that she couldn't have gone very far. Yet, Con found no sight of her, the mare, or the cart anywhere.

He tried another direction. And another. And another.

Until he finally realized that somehow, she had disappeared.

Still, he looked for another two hours before returning to Dreagan. He waited until he was once more in the mountain before he shifted into his human form. He dressed and walked back to his office where he sat behind his desk and pulled out his journal. He turned to a blank page and dipped his quill in ink.

Con wished that Nikolai had seen Heather, because he could've drawn her. Now it was up to him to do his best in recreating her image. Con began with the shape of her face and then her eyes. Next was her hair, and then her body.

When he finished, he stared down at the page and sighed. It was a fair likeness of the lass, and while there was still a nugget of worry within him, he had a sense that whoever Heather was, she didn't want to harm the Kings.

That didn't mean Constantine wasn't going to be ready in case there was an attack.

Ever.

He dipped his quill again, and on the opposite page, began a new journal entry.

The 13th of August, human year 1601

Yesterday began as any other until I met an extraordinary woman named Heather. I don't know who she is, or even what she is, but I spent a most pleasant afternoon in her company.

While her beauty is unparalleled, it is her mind that truly intrigues me. I suspected early on that she might know who we are at Dreagan. Despite many attempts while she was with me and once she departed, I was unable to piece together who she might be.

The fact that she drew Roman's attention as well brought Banan to my office where he pointed out the spell we used to prevent us from having feelings for mortals. I hate to admit it, but I had not thought of it. Thanks to Banan, it made me realize that Heather was most likely not human.

So I went looking for her.

Despite my keen dragon vision and hours of searching, I found no trace of Heather. If Roman had not met her, I might believe she had been a ghost. But I know she was real.

I will find her again. There are many questions I have for her. The first one is discovering her true identity.

Constantine, the King of Golds
King of Dragon Kings

The rain fell upon his upturned face steadily, the drops beating against his skin in a rhythm he knew well. Con opened his eyes and looked to the heavens to see dozens of dragons flying over him. For just a heartbeat, he could almost believe the dragons had returned.

But there were no flocks of clans dotting the horizon. Just the Dragon Kings who remained behind to stop the war and give the other dragons a chance at survival on a new world.

The thunderstorm that rolled in at dawn gave the Kings a chance to take to the skies during the day. Thunder masked their roars. While Con was happy to see his brethren flying, it was bittersweet since it had been many, many years since any of them had felt the sun upon their scales.

Still, it was better than not being able to fly at all. Because Con knew that day would come eventually. Something would happen that would ground all the Kings. He wasn't looking forward to that day, but there was no running from it. And once that came, it would only be a matter of time before there was another war – possibly the last war.

"Con."

He lowered his face and turned to Asher behind him. The Dragon King's green eyes held a dose of concern. Con shoved his long, wet hair out of his face and blinked against the rain as he made his way to Asher.

"What is it?" Con asked.

Asher jerked his dark head toward the manor. "A package was delivered just now."

"From who?"

Asher shrugged. "The lad who brought it said he had instructions to deliver it this morning."

Without another word, Asher shifted, shredding his clothes. Con watched the large hunter green dragon take to the sky to join the others before he walked to the manor. Inside, he removed his sodden clothing and walked naked to the foyer where a small package sat on the table.

He took it, studying it for a moment. Then, he pulled on the ribbon strings to unwrap it and reveal a wooden box. Con couldn't image what could be inside a box that fit within the palm of his hand. His curiosity was too great, however, and he opened the lid.

His gaze landed on two small gold dragon heads. He lifted one, inspecting the flawless design while detecting no magic. It wasn't until he returned the petite dragon head to the box that he saw the folded paper tucked into the lid. Con set the box on the table and removed the paper, slowly unfolding it to read.

Constantine –

I will never forget my time at Dreagan. It was truly an amazing day that I'll look back on fondly in the days to come. Just as I will when I think of you.

I made these cuff links for you after seeing all the dragons around the manor. These are for you to replace the ribbons at your wrist that you detest so. I hope when you wear them, they remind you to let go of the past and to focus on your goals.

H

He folded the paper and tucked it back in the lid before taking the box and making his way to his room. There he dressed before reaching for the cuff links. As soon as he put them in place, he smiled. He suspected he just found an item that he would wear for centuries to come.

Whether Heather knew he was the King of Golds or not, she had chosen perfectly. And it made him want to find her more than ever.

He adjusted his sleeves, running his fingers over the cuff links, before he strode from the room. The hunt for Heather was on.

Death

Being Death had its positive sides, but they were rare. Erith knew it was a huge gamble to meet Constantine, but she was tired of watching him and the other Dragon Kings. She wanted – *needed* – to be in the mix. Even if it was only briefly.

The dragons were as old as time – and so was she. Though the first few million years she spent being something else, something she hadn't been proud of. But through many trials, she eventually found her true self.

It was watching the Dragon Kings, specifically Con, that had begun to change her way of thinking. From there, she made the decision to be a different person. Though one thing remained the same – her solitude. She couldn't be Death and be surrounded by friends. There were things she had to do that were better done on her own.

Few could understand that better than Con. The King of Dragon Kings might even have it worse than she did.

While she remained a part from others, he was surrounded by other Dragon Kings, never allowing himself to get too close to any of his brethren. It was the bane of a leader. In order to make the right decisions, many times, personal feelings had to be taken out of the equation.

No one did that better than Constantine.

His focus had always been on the dragons and saving them, even when he was fighting for his life with Ulrik – his best friend.

It nearly killed Erith not to get involved between the two of them, but she had kept her distance. In the end, it was Con's love for his friend that prevented him from ending Ulrik's life.

Some could argue that it was Con's greatest mistake. In her eyes, it proved how great a leader he was. Despite the threat that Ulrik could one day come for him, Con did what was in his heart.

Talking to the King of Kings, getting to know him had been a real treat. She hated lying to him and giving him a false name, but she wasn't ready for any of the Dragon Kings to know of her existence. The Fae were her focus.

At least she had bestowed a gift upon Con. Gold from the deepest mountains. Dragons she personally carved. And a sincere wish that they would bring him some sort of peace in the tumultuous years to come.

For an untold number of eons, she hadn't just been judge and jury to the Fae – both Dark and Light – she had been their executioner as well. It was while watching one of the many battles between the Fae that she came across a warrior who captured her attention.

He fought as if he were waging war on his own. His skills were incredible, his blade lethal. He was one that others looked up to and followed. And then he was betrayed by those closest to him and killed.

When the last breath left his body, she went to him and gave him an offer. If he carried out her punishments without question, she would return his life. In service to her as a Reaper, he would be given more power than before. He had accepted.

The creation of her Reapers was the missing part of her journey. Erith couldn't believe she had gone so long without them. They were an extension of her. Now, she was the judge and jury, but the Reapers were the executioners.

And it hadn't taken long for them to become feared. More so, because part of their promise was that no Fae could ever know their identities.

She teleported into a rainstorm on a tiny isle in the middle of the loch and found the Fae doorway. Once through it, she smiled as the sunlight beat down on her. The songs of birds filled the air along with the heady smell of the various flowers.

Erith stopped next to a group of wild heather that was a symbol of Scotland. And since the Dragon Kings made Scotland there home, the choice in her alias had been easy. She studied the hearty, fast growing plant with its purple blooms. The flower had many uses in the Scottish culture, and not surprisingly, even the Druids considered it a sacred plant.

She gave one last look to the heather before moving to the various roses to inhale their heady fragrance. Daisies were another particular favorite of hers, as were dahlias. And acacia, violets, irises, and jasmine.

Then again, there wasn't a flower she didn't love. They were all stunning in their unique way. The blossoms brought beauty and simplicity into her realm.

The plain clothes she wore to meet Con disappeared, replaced with a long black gown. The full skirt brushed against the plants as she walked down the path. She released her hair from the braid and let it fall loose to her hips while butterflies danced around her and dragonflies zoomed ahead of her in a wild, beautiful dance to welcome her back.

The white tower that was her home gleamed in the sunlight like a beacon. She made her way toward it. Meeting Con had set things in motion, things that she now couldn't undo. She hoped she'd made the right decision.

For herself, for the Reapers – and the Dragon Kings.

And for what was to come.

Thank you for reading **Constantine: A History**. I hope you enjoyed getting to know a little more about Con, the Dragon Kings, Death, and the Reapers and how they've been tied together for a long time.

If you liked this book – or any of my other releases – please consider rating the book at the online retailer of your choice. Your ratings and reviews help other readers find new favorites, and of course there is no better or more appreciated support for an author than word of mouth recommendations from happy readers. Thanks again for your interest in my books!

Donna Grant

www.DonnaGrant.com
www.MotherofDragonsBooks.com

DARK ALPHA'S CLAIM

The Reapers Series, Book 1

Jordyn Patterson stepped to the side to dodge a man hurrying down the narrow aisle with a cup of coffee. She rolled her eyes and made her way to her desk.

She'd barely sat down and rolled her chair into place when her boss, Detective Inspector Dougal MacDonald walked from his office to stand by her desk.

"It's been a few days since the American, Lexi Crawford, has been in. Did she make her way home?" he asked.

Jordyn gave a nod. "I made sure I'd get notified by the airline when she checked in. She's back in South Carolina now, sir."

"Good. Good," he said again with a nod. "Too much craziness has been going on in this town. At least the killings have stopped. That's a relief."

Jordyn merely smiled as he walked away. She never told MacDonald her thoughts, because they went against everything he was. From the first time Lexi Crawford came into the station and repeated her story to MacDonald in her southern accent, Jordyn had been enthralled.

Red eyes! She hadn't believed Lexi either at first. MacDonald dismissed Lexi's story as nonsense, but Jordyn felt the need to look deeper into the case. Especially when more and more people were being killed every night.

There had been a day—only a few hours really—when everyone whispered about red eyes.

Jordyn went home and frantically searched through the mountain of books she accumulated on the Fae. She read in one that some of the Fae had red eyes.

She stayed up all night looking for

that passage. An hour before dawn, she finally found it. Jordyn had sat on the floor with the open book in hand and stared numbly.

For as long as she could remember, the Fae were talked about in her family. Sometimes when someone did something unique and amazing, her family would say it was because of the Fae within them.

Other times when someone did something horrible, the Fae were mentioned with words laced in fear.

Jordyn's curiosity about the Fae grew as she did, until it consumed her. She began researching them when she was thirteen. Now, twenty years later, she was still gathering information about them, only she was doing it in Edinburgh hours away from her family. There was really only so much a person could do in a small village. Jordyn had needed a city.

She knew the Fae were real. There couldn't be that many stories—folktales or otherwise—without the beings being real. However, she had yet to meet one.

Over the last five years, she'd begun to try and discover how to find the Fae. She thought she would have to do all sorts of tricks to see one, but it seemed that all she had to do was go out on the streets of Edinburgh.

The very next day she had, and she'd been shaken to her very core. Every book she read described the Fae differently, from tiny winged creatures to giants. She didn't know what to expect, but the sheer number of Fae walking around with red eyes gave her pause.

Then she saw them killing. And it wasn't with a knife or gun. They killed with sex.

Jordyn shuddered in her chair. She'd been hunting the Fae for most of her life. What she found made her wish she didn't know of them.

But they were the dark side of the Fae. Dark Fae to be exact. Their use of glamour aside, they had red eyes and their black hair had silver in it.

Some of the Dark had more silver than others, and that gave her pause. She wanted to think it meant they were older, but she suspected it meant something else entirely.

Their laughter as they killed human after human made her ill. She ran away that night and ducked behind an alley to empty her stomach.

After that, she desperately wanted Lexi to come into the station again and tell MacDonald more of what she had seen, but Lexi didn't return.

For a while, Jordyn began to suspect that Lexi was dead with dozens of other humans. Then the notice from the airline came, and Jordyn breathed a sigh of relief.

Halloween was the worst. Even now, a few days later, it still appeared as if the Fae had a hold on the city. Most of them were gone, but she could tell where a Dark was just by where the men and women gathered, fawning over them as they tried to get close.

Jordyn didn't know why she wasn't drawn to the Dark like everyone else, but she was glad she wasn't. Perhaps it was all she'd read about the Fae. Despite not knowing what was true and what was fiction, she did know they were real.

A glance at the clock confirmed she had a few hours before she could take her lunch. Jordyn came across mention of a book that might shed more light on the Fae.

She tried to purchase it, but no one had it. It was fortunate that she called the library and they actually had a copy.

The new librarian, however, was a bit of a prude and refused to hold the book for her until after work. If Jordyn wanted it, she was going to have to race over there during her lunch.

She kept busy until noon, then Jordyn grabbed her purse and hurried from the office. She flagged a taxi and gave the address. There wasn't much time to get to the library and return to work before lunch ended.

Normally she would walk, but it was too far away. She'd never make it back in time. Jordyn drummed her fingers on the door of the taxi as it drew to a halt at a stoplight. Every second spent sitting still was a second wasted.

Her stomach rumbled in hunger. If she were lucky, she would be able to grab some chips and stuff a few in her mouth before she was back at her desk.

By the time the taxi pulled up to the library, Jordyn was anxious to get out. She threw a few bills at the driver as she opened the door and said, "Keep the rest."

She ran up the steps as a gust of wind barreled down the street. Jordyn pulled her arms tight against her, wishing she hadn't forgotten her coat.

The man exiting the library saw her but didn't hold the door open. She shook her head. Where were the men who held doors and were still gentlemen? Apparently, they went the way of the dodo bird.

"Jerk," she mumbled beneath her breath as she entered the library.

As soon as she stepped inside, Jordyn smiled. There was a special smell to a library. It was leather, wood, and the pages of books.

She'd always had a love of books. The feel of the weight of it in her hand, the smell of the pages, the words written that could give her facts or take her off on a visual story.

Now wasn't the time to wander the aisles though. Jordyn walked up to the counter. "Excuse me. I have a book being held."

"Your name?" the woman asked without turning around.

Jordyn frowned at the back of her. It was like the woman studied what a librarian should be and copied it from the tight bun, the glasses, and the frumpy, plain clothes. "Jordyn Patterson."

The woman looked at her watch. "With just a few minutes to spare." She bent and pulled out the book from the beneath the counter and turned, setting it down beside her.

Jordyn was taken aback at the woman. She was pretty with her dark hair and pale blue eyes. Not at all what she expected with such a bitchy voice from the phone, or the image she got from the back of her in her prim button-down, cardigan, and long, plaid skirt.

"Here," she said, handing the card over to Jordyn to sign out the book.

Once she filled it out, Jordyn pulled the book into her arms. "Thanks for holding it."

"You have two weeks. The book will need to be returned then," the librarian said as she met Jorydn's gaze.

"Yep." Jordyn turned her back on the woman and rolled her eyes.

Had she been able to find the book

online, she wouldn't have had to deal with the librarian from Hell. If the book held as much information as Jordyn hoped it did, she was going to have to widen her search for it, because a book like it belonged in her own library, not the city's, where no one would check it out.

Jordyn fought the urge to open the book as she walked down the steps of the building. By the time she reached the bottom, her will crumpled. She had it open and was flipping through pages in a heartbeat.

Her eyes scanned page after page as her brain soaked up everything. Jordyn couldn't wait to get home and begin making notes.

With her stomach rumbling again, Jordyn turned to find some food when she ran into someone. Her shoulder was jarred so that she nearly lost her hold on the book. "Sorry," she said and looked up into the most amazing silver eyes.

"Must be an interesting book," he said.

She nodded, unable to find words for a moment. The man was the most gorgeous person she'd ever seen. Her reaction to him was instantaneous, earth-shattering.

He was mouth-wateringly gorgeous, heart-stoppingly magnificent. His short coal black hair was wavy and full. Her fingers itched to run through the locks and see if they felt as shiny as they looked.

His beautiful face was lean and hard, with his chiseled jaw and chin. Not to mention his wide, thin lips. His gaze was direct, intense. Relentless.

While he sized her up, she let her gaze fall to his chest. An olive green long-sleeved tee showed off broad shoulders and arms that rippled with muscles. She imagined when he took off that shirt that he would be toned and supple, with just the right amount of hard sinew. Black jeans were slung low on his narrow hips with black boots completing his look.

"It is," she finally answered when she looked back up into his face.

"Fae, huh?" He glanced down at the page before his silver eyes returned to hers.

His gaze was molten, holding her still and making her blood heat. The desire, the yearning to have his lips on hers made her heart skip a beat and her stomach flutter.

Jordyn had never felt such attraction before. Another gust of wind hit her, but she didn't feel the chill. Her body was too heated.

That's when she registered the Irish accent. "Research."

"Good luck with your research," he said and bowed his head.

Jordyn had the urge to stay and talk to him, but her stomach growled, reminding her she had little time to get food and make it back to the office. She reluctantly walked away from the handsome Irishman to the pub down the street.

It was the first time in a long time that she actually wanted to interact with a man, because the Irishman knocked her off her feet with just a few words and an intense look from his silver eyes.

In no time, she had an order of chips to go. With food in hand, she hailed another taxi and gobbled the grease-soaked potatoes and flipped through the book. Though she found herself looking out her window for another glimpse of the Irishman.

It was the worst sort of punishment to have to put the book away and get back to work. The day crawled as she constantly looked at the clock, waiting for her workday to end so she could get to her research.

Baylon was sitting on the steps outside the library watching the mortals when he saw her. She stood out amongst the humans like a star in the midnight sky.

Her beauty was undeniable, catching the attention of everyone around her - though she didn't seem to notice. He liked the way her dark blond hair was cut short and trendy with it swept to the side in the front. A pixie cut, he thought he heard a human call it.

The mortal was tall and thin, with every curve just the right size. Her turquoise eyes were large, and there was a hint of innocence about them that drew him again and again.

She wore large earrings that brought more attention to her beautiful oval face. Her brows were thin and arched delicately over her eyes. When she smiled, she dazzled. Her lips were just wide and full enough to be alluring.

He'd laughed when he heard her mumble "jerk" to the man who hadn't held the door for her.

He knew immediately that she had

Fae blood. It wasn't just her beauty. There was an air about her that was as distinctive as a beacon. And he was happy he found her before the others.

Baylon waited outside the library for another glimpse of her. She walked out a short time later carrying a large book. She was entranced by it. Several people had to walk around her because she wasn't looking where she was going— she was too intent on reading.

He wanted to see what kind of book was so interesting. When he put himself in her path, he never expected to look down at a tome all about the Fae.

His shock was quickly replaced with a blinding and penetrating desire when they bumped into each other. Then she looked up at him.

He was completely taken by her, tumbling into incredible turquoise eyes.

If he didn't speak, he was liable to do something stupid—like kiss her. His gaze lowered to her lips, an ache gripping him, begging him to take her.

To taste her.

"Sorry," she said.

Her Scots accent was soft and lilting. Beautiful, just as she was. What was it about this half-Fae that held him enthralled so? "Must be an interesting book."

Her gaze slowly raked over him, heating his blood to such a degree that he fisted his hands to keep from touching her. Didn't she realize she was playing with fire?

If her gaze wasn't so guileless, Baylon would have suspected she was proficient in teasing a man to such a degree. But it was the need in her own eyes that made his cock instantly hard.

"It is."

He glanced down at the page she was reading. "Fae, huh?"

"Research," she said breathlessly.

Warning bells went off in Baylon's head. Research? Did she know she had Fae blood? It was time he found out more about her. Besides, he was going to make sure none of the other Reapers found her.

"Good luck with your research." He bowed his head and walked around her.

He then stopped and turned to watch her, wondering if she would look back at him. To his exasperation, she didn't.

Baylon veiled himself and followed her all the way to the police station. From there, he watched her. She was friendly and always had a smile. Everyone liked her.

She didn't give anyone a second look, preferring to concentrate on her work. She was quick and accurate in everything she did.

Baylon wondered if she knew how the others looked at her, watched her. She was graceful and striking without being flamboyant. She had her own kind of elegance that screamed Fae.

But mortals wouldn't know that.

To another Fae, it was like a beacon.

He'd stumbled onto a half-Fae

without even trying. Fate couldn't be that cruel to him, surely. There was something about the order from Death that was just wrong. Humans, even those with Fae blood, had never been targeted by the Reapers.

Perhaps Baylon needed to have a talk with Cael. Disobeying Death's orders wasn't an option, but that's exactly what Baylon was going to do for the time being. It felt wrong to target half-Fae.

He was about to leave to find Cael, but then the mortal smiled. She was safe. The others weren't in the area, so they wouldn't be looking for her.

Why then wasn't Baylon leaving?

Because he couldn't. A feeling in his gut kept him right where he was, continuing to watch her. He found it humorous as just about every man in the station tried to get her attention while all the women made a point of talking to her.

The humans couldn't help it. It was

the Fae blood within the mortal that
drew them.

   Just as she captivated him.

ABOUT DONNA GRANT

New York Times and *USA Today* bestselling author Donna Grant has been praised for her "totally addictive" and "unique and sensual" stories. She's written more than seventy novels spanning multiple genres of romance including the bestselling Dark King stories. Her acclaimed series, Dark Warriors, feature a thrilling combination of Druids, primeval gods, and immortal Highlanders who are dark, dangerous, and irresistible. She lives with two children, a dog, and three cats in Texas.

www.DonnaGrant.com

www.MotherofDragonsBooks.com

Newsletter: tinyurl.com/DonnaGrantNews

Text Updates:

text DRAGONKING to 24587

Facebook: AuthorDonnaGrant

Facebook Reader Group:

http://bit.ly/DGGroupies

Twitter: donna_grant

Instagram: DGAuthor

Pinterest: DonnaGrant1

Bookbub: http://bit.ly/2siVQKK

Amazon: http://amzn.to/2f8xeP0

Goodreads: http://bit.ly/2vinVCD

Spotify Book Playlists:

http://bit.ly/donnagrant_author

Made in the USA
Monee, IL
18 April 2022

94979380R00066